Arnold Neimanis

CHARLOTTE CAFFEY is a singer-songwriter best known for being a member of the all-female new wave group the Go-Go's. Caffey wrote the hit single "We Got the Beat," and has cowritten songs for other artists such as Keith Urban as well as the theme song for the television series *Clueless.* The Go-Go's became one of the foundational bands of the 1980s, with their 1981 debut album *Beauty and the Beat* going double platinum and topping the US *Billboard* charts for six weeks. The band has sold more than seven million records across the world. Caffey continues to write and perform.

KAITLYN SHEA O'CONNOR (illustrator) is an illustrator and designer hailing from Atlanta, Georgia. She combines traditional skills with digital media to create vibrant, whimsical worlds. She's a rare hybrid of dog and cat lover, an avid whistler, and she enjoys exploring the great outdoors, trying new cheeses, and cozying up in a nook with a book. Discover more of her work at designedbyshea.com.

"We Got the Beat"
Written by Charlotte Caffey
Courtesy of Universal Music—MGB Songs
Used by Permission. All Rights Reserved.

LyricPop is a children's picture book collection by LyricVerse and Akashic Books.

lyricverse

Published by Akashic Books
Song lyrics ©1981 Charlotte Caffey
Illustrations ©2020 Kaitlyn Shea O'Connor

ISBN: 978-1-61775-836-2
Library of Congress Control Number: 2020935753
First printing

Printed in China

Akashic Books
Brooklyn, New York
Twitter: @AkashicBooks
Facebook: AkashicBooks
E-mail: info@akashicbooks.com
Website: www.akashicbooks.com

We Got the Beat

SONG LYRICS BY
CHARLOTTE CAFFEY

ILLUSTRATIONS BY KAITLYN SHEA O'CONNOR

AKASHIC BOOKS LYRICPOP

See the people walking down the street

Fall in LINE just watchin' all their feet

They don't **KNOW** where they want to **go**
But they're **WALKIN'** in **tiMe**

They got the beat

They got the beat

They got the beat

YEAH, THEY GOT THE BEAT

All the KiDS just gettin' out of SCHooL

They can't wait to HaNG out and be CooL

Hang around till quarter after TweLve

That's when they fall in LiNe

Yeah, KIDS GOT THE BEAT

Go-Go music really makes us DaNCe

Do the PONY puts us in a tRaNCe

Do what you SEE just give us a CHaNCE

That's when they fall in LiNe

'Cause we got the BEAt

We got the BEaT

We got the
BeAt

We got the
BeAt

We got the BEAT

EVER

GET on y

(we GOT TH

BODY

ur FeEt

(EAT)

(We got the BEAT)

ROUND
and
ROUND
and ROUND

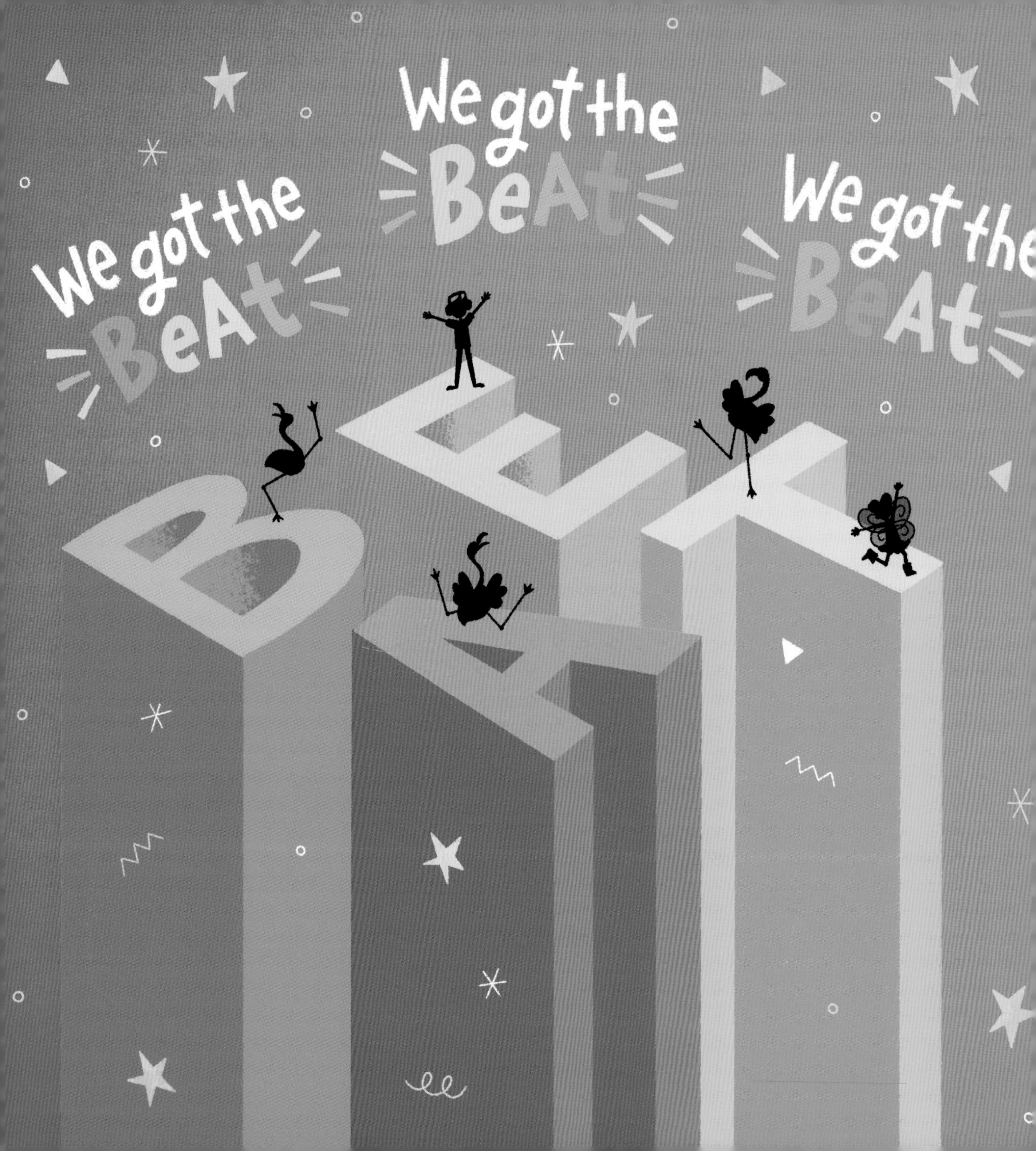
We got the BeAt
We got the BeAt
We got the BeAt
BEAT

LOOK OUT FOR THESE LyricPop TITLES

African SONG LYRICS BY PETER TOSH
ILLUSTRATIONS BY RACHEL MOSS

(Sittin' on) The Dock of the Bay
SONG LYRICS BY OTIS REDDING AND STEVE CROPPER
ILLUSTRATIONS BY KAITLYN SHEA O'CONNOR

Don't Stop SONG LYRICS BY CHRISTINE MCVIE
ILLUSTRATIONS BY NUSHA ASHJAEE

Good Vibrations
SONG LYRICS BY MIKE LOVE AND BRIAN WILSON
ILLUSTRATIONS BY PAUL HOPPE

Humble and Kind SONG LYRICS BY LORI MCKENNA
ILLUSTRATIONS BY KATHERINE BLACKMORE

Move the Crowd
SONG LYRICS BY ERIC BARRIER AND WILLIAM GRIFFIN
ILLUSTRATIONS BY KIRK PARRISH

Respect SONG LYRICS BY OTIS REDDING
ILLUSTRATIONS BY RACHEL MOSS

These Boots Are Made for Walkin'
SONG LYRICS BY LEE HAZLEWOOD, ILLUSTRATIONS BY RACHEL MOSS

We're Not Gonna Take It SONG LYRICS BY DEE SNIDER
ILLUSTRATIONS BY MARGARET MCCARTNEY

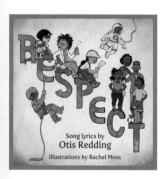

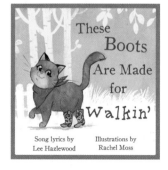